VIKRAM
AND BETAL

Contents

King Vikram
and the Sage

A long time ago, India was ruled by a king called Vikram. He was known for his courage and wisdom. His people loved him dearly as he was a just king. King Vikram ensured that everyone in his kingdom was happy.

One day, while King Vikram was holding court, a sage came to ask for his help. King Vikram promised to help him.

So he asked the king to meet him in the cremation ground outside the city on the next moonless night.

Although the king was puzzled by this strange request, he set out to meet the sage, as he had already given his word.

When the sage saw him, he said, "My brave king, deep in the forest there is an old peepul tree, from which a corpse hangs upside down. Please bring that corpse to me."

King Vikram set out in search of the peepul tree, spotted the tree and the corpse hanging from it.

He dragged the corpse down and slung it over his shoulder.

Just then, the corpse let out a blood-curdling laugh. The king was taken aback. He realised that the corpse was not an ordinary corpse. It was a ghost.

Undeterred, he purposefully walked on. Hardly had he taken a few steps when the corpse escaped from his shoulder and went back to the peepul tree. King Vikram walked back to the tree.

He brought down the corpse, and started walking out of the forest. "Who are you?" asked King Vikram.

"I am Betal," the corpse replied. "Where are we going?"

"A sage asked me to take you to him," replied the king.

"Well, I will go with you on one condition," said the corpse. "Since it is a long walk, I shall tell you a story to pass the time. But if you speak, I shall fly back to the tree."

King Vikram agreed to the conditions laid down by the corpse. So he carried him on his back, and they continued their journey.

Of the Marvellous Delicacy of Three Queens

Vikram walked back to the tree and caught hold of Betal. With determination, he walked on hoping that Betal would not speak. But Betal soon began a new story.

One day, King Dharmadhwaj decided to go for a stroll. He was accompanied by three of his beautiful queens. Soon, he came upon a large tank filled with lovely blooming lotuses. The Raja captivated by its beauty, took off his clothes and went to bathe in the water.

After plucking a flower, he came to the bank. As he offered one queen a flower, it fell on her foot and crushed it. Alarmed, the King set about trying to heal the wounds. When night arrived, the Raja and his second queen went outdoors.

The moon's rays fell on her body and formed blisters. The worried Raja tried everything to get her cured.

Later in the day, the noise of a wooden pestle came from afar. At this, the third queen fainted with a bad headache. The Raja was miserable.

Then, Betal stopped abruptly. "Now, Vikram," he said, "which of the queens was most delicate?"

"The one who fainted because of a headache was the most delicate," answered Vikram, and Betal went back to the peepul tree.

In Which a Man Deceives a Woman

After grabbing Betal once again, Vikram started walking out of the forest. Betal then began another story.

Once, there lived a handsome prince, Vajramukut. One day, he went hunting with his friends but got separated. Then he came across a beautiful princess. Upon seeing him, she screamed angrily for her maids who made him leave. But the prince had impressed her deeply. Meanwhile, he returned to his friends and told them about the princess. As he wished to meet her, the minister's son suggested that they go find the princess. They set off in disguise.

Soon, they stopped to rest at an old woman's home. "I am the nurse of Princess Padmavati whom you seek," she said. She welcomed her guests to stay with her.

Once, the prince gave her a message to take to the princess. But when she took it to

the princess, the princess tore it up, and cursed her. The nurse returned to the unhappy prince.

"Be not so hasty," said the minister's crafty son. "She has not rejected you yet."

The old nurse decided to try again. But again, the princess was angry and slapped her.

"By hitting the old woman, she has agreed to meet you," said the minister's son calmly.

Soon Padmavati and Vajramukut chanced to meet. The proud Padmavati disliked his daring manner and secretly vowed to revenge herself.

Vajramukut told the minister's son of the princess's behaviour. Then the friend said, "Listen, I have a plan. When the princess is asleep, feed her this powder. Then strike her left leg. Take her jewels to the bazaar the very next day."

So Vajramukut went about his plan. But at the bazaar, the chief jeweller recognised the jewels. Vajramukut was taken to the king. "Oh King," Vajramukut said. "I found them in a cemetery with a witch. I hit her leg with my trident and took off these jewels."

Stunned, Raja Dantawat called his mother and said, "Mother, go check whether there are any strange marks on Padmavati's leg."

His mother found this to be true.

The king's heart sank at this news but he decided that Padmavati would be banished as punishment. The plan had suceeded. The poor girl then agreed to marry Vajramukut.

"Now, Raja Vikram," said Betal, "who was to blame really?"

"King Dantawat," said Vikram. "The wise and experienced Raja should not have been deceived by such a silly trick."

Then, Betal flew back to the tree.

Of the Relative Villainy of Men and Women

Vikram caught Betal once again. But soon Betal began his storytelling.

There once lived a pleasure-loving and careless king. When he died, he left an empty treasury for his son. But he had a wise parrot, Churaman. Soon, the new king got married.

His new bride, Chandravati also had a clever jay. Once the Raja and Chandravati sat down with their birds. Now the jay disliked all males.

When the Raja asked for a story, the jay obliged, "Once, there was a rich merchant. He had a son who was a hunchback. After his father died, he visited my master, and narrated a false tale about his life. My master was deceived. In time, his daughter Ratnavati married the hunchback.

One day, the hunchback wished to go to his city. Ratnavati went with him. In the forest, he threw Ratnavati into a well. A passerby rescued her and escorted her home.

Soon, the hunchback too came to his wife's home. He was shocked to see his wife alive. His wife forgave him and they lived peacefully, till one day, the hunchback killed my master, his wife and Ratnavati. He was about to kill me when the barking of a dog distracted him."

The jay burst into tears. All were silent. The king asked Churaman to tell a tale.

"Once, I belonged to a rich merchant. He had a spoilt daughter, Jayashri, who had married her friend, Shridat. One night, she secretly went to visit an admirer. On reaching his home, she found him dead. All the while, one of the king's footmen had followed her.

Now as Jayashri wept beside her admirer's body, an evil spirit entered the dead man and bit off her nose. Screaming, she ran home. When she saw Shridat, she shrieked wildly, clasping her nose.

The noise brought the neighbours out of their houses. And Shridat was taken to the king. Then, the footman cried, 'Oh King, this man is innocent.' He narrated the true events and the wicked Jayashri was then punished."

The jay was outraged by the story of the evil woman. The jay and parrot began to fight. Soon all four were arguing.

"A man may know right and wrong but a woman does not," said the Raja crossly. To his dismay, Betal flew away to the tree.

Of the Use and Misuse of Magic Pills

Raja Vikram walked back to the tree, took down the corpse and placed him on his shoulders. Betal started to tell a new story.

Raja Subichar had a beautiful daughter, Chandraprabha. One day, the princess went for a walk in the forest nearby. It so happened that just then Manaswi, a handsome brahmin youth came there. He sat down to rest under a tree. The princess too came there to rest. On seeing Manaswi, she was startled.

Both the Raja's daughter and Manaswi fainted. The princess' attendants carried her home. Two brahmins, Muldev and Shashi then saw Manaswi.

When Manaswi awoke, he told them his story. Muldev took him to his house. "I have a secret weapon to help you realise your dream of meeting the princess. Place this magic pill in your mouth and you will become a girl. Then, do as I say. But beware do not misuse it," he said.

Manaswi agreed to this. Then, they went to the Raja's palace. "Oh King," Muldev said, "my village was struck by famine while I was away. I found a bride for my son but my family has gone. Look after her till I find them."

So Manaswi, as Sita, came to stay with Chandraprabha. That evening, Sita removed the pill from her mouth and changed into Manaswi. Chandraprabha, confused, blushed furiously.

Manaswi and the princess were happy but they dared not reveal the truth to the Raja.

One day, they went to a feast. There, the treasurer's son fell in love with Sita. The minister then brought his son's marriage proposal which the king refused angrily, fearing the brahmin's curse. He returned empty-handed to his son. But the crafty minister knew that the king would have to relent as he could not run the kingdom without his help. But the king too would rather die than break a promise.

Finally the King was forced to submit to his treasurer's request. Both Chandraprabha and Sita got scared when they heard the news. "Great King!" said Sita, "I request that he perform a yatra to all the holy places before I accept the marriage proposal." The king agreed and the treasurer's son was sent on a pilgrimage.

One night, the magic pill went down Manaswi's throat before he could change back into Sita. So he had to escape from the palace. The news reached Shashi and Muldev.

"I told you that he was a cheat. Now remember, you promised the princess' hand in marriage to me if I was right about him." said Shashi.

So, Muldev gave the magic pill to old Shashi, who changed into a young Brahman. The two went to the Raja, who recognised Muldev at once.

The Raja told him all that had happened. Muldev asked, "Raja, what have you done? Now, I ask that you give your daughter to my son here or else suffer my curse."

The Raja agreed and the two were married. When Manaswi heard this, he went to Shashi, saying that he had married Chandraprabha. But, she denied it outright. Many believed Manaswi's story as it was so incredible.

"Foolish people!" cried Vikram, who hated elopements. "Shashi married her lawfully and she is therefore his wife."

Then, Betal flew away. Vikram went back to the tree, and pulled down Betal again.

Too Much Charity

Betal began his story, as King Vikram briskly walked through the forest.

Once upon a time, there lived an extremely rich man. He was very careful with his money. He had a very honest and well-meaning servant, Nageshwar.

One day, Nageshwar asked his master for some money. He assured him that the money would be well-spent. Initially, his master was reluctant.

But upon hearing Nageshwar's assurances, he agreed and gave his servant ten gold coins but told him not to reveal the source of the money.

Nageshwar agreed. With the money, he built a small resting place for travellers.

Nageshwar's efforts pleased his master. So the next time Nageshwar asked for money, he was given fifty gold coins.

With this money, Nageshwar built a free lodge for travellers and the poor. Everyone praised Nageshwar's efforts.

After some time, Nageshwar asked for money again. He wanted to provide free food for those staying at his inn. His master readily gave it to him.

Gradually, the inn began to expand. More and more was spent on its maintenance.

One day, the rich man died, putting an end to Nageshwar's income. So he was forced to ask the travellers to pay up. This created a lot of discontentment among them. Once a few agitated travellers attacked Nageshwar and killed him.

Then, Betal asked, "Who killed Nageshwar? Speak up now, or else your head will be blown up into a thousand pieces."

King Vikram promptly answered, "Actually, Nageshwar alone was the cause of his death. If he had charged the travellers from the beginning, he would have been spared an untimely death. He should have known that the source of the money would not last forever."

"Your answer is correct but you have broken your promise of not speaking," said Betal, and he flew back to the peepul tree.

The Most Noble of All

King Vikram was determined to keep his word about delivering the corpse. So he went back to the peepul tree, pulled Betal down, slung him across his shoulders, and started his journey again. But Betal started narrating another story.

Once, a minister saw a beautiful girl in a temple. Entranced by her beauty, he sent his servant to find out about her.

"Her name is Anjali and she is the daughter of a rich merchant of this city," the minister was told.

The minister went to Anjali's father and spoke of his desire to marry her but he learnt that her marriage had already been fixed. The minister was heartbroken. Anjali felt overwhelmed by the minister's love. She promised to meet him once again.

After her wedding, Anjali told her husband, Chandradeep about her promise to the minister.

Chandradeep allowed her to meet him, so Anjali set out for the minister's house, alone.

On the way, she had to pass through a jungle. Just then, a thief attacked her. Anjali begged him to let her go, and promised to give him all her jewellery on her way back. He believed her and let her go.

When Anjali reached the minister's house, it was dark.

According to the law if a man was seen with a married lady after dark, he would be punished. The minister was shocked to see Anjali that night. He was rude to her. Humiliated, Anjali left for home.

On her way back, Anjali met the thief again. After taking her jewellery, he asked her why she was alone in the forest. Anjali told him her story.

After hearing her story, the thief was touched by her honesty and did not rob her. Instead, he escorted her back home.

When Anjali returned home, she told her husband everything that had happened that night. But her husband did not believe her.

In his anger, he sent Anjali away. Anjali was beside herself with grief and she committed suicide.

Then Betal stopped. "Tell me," he said, "who was the most noble? Answer me, or else your head will burst into pieces!"

Vikram replied, "Anjali committed suicide as she feared the rejection and the humiliation. All the characters had selfish motives except the thief. He could have robbed Anjali, but he did not. He was the most noble."

At these words, Betal flew back to the tree.

The Greatest Sacrifice

King Vikram never gave up easily. He walked back to the peepul tree, brought the corpse down, put it on his shoulders and walked on. Betal soon began to narrate another story.

Once, there lived a king. He had a faithful guard called Virsen. Virsen was a brave and devoted man. While on duty, he was always vigilant and alert. He had a wife, a son and a daughter.

One day, while he was on duty guarding the palace gates, he heard someone crying loudly. The king, too, woke up from his deep slumber, looking concerned. He then sent for Virsen and told him to find out who was crying in the middle of the night.

Virsen did as he was told. Soon he found that it was a woman crying. When asked, the woman said, "I am the goddess of good fortune. The king was under my protection. But now an evil spirit has overpowered me, and the king will die within three days."

After hearing this horrifying news, Virsen was determined to protect his master. He learnt that the only way was by sacrificing his own son to Goddess Kali.

Virsen rushed home and related the incident to his family. "I am ready to die, Father," his son said. "Take me to the temple."

Without wasting much time, his family went to the Kali temple. After seeing her brother sacrificed at the altar, Virsen's daughter was heartbroken, and unable to bear the pain of separation from her brother, she too died. Virsen's wife was shocked to see both her children lying dead before her. So, she too killed herself, as she did not wish to live without her beloved children. Seeing

his family dead before him, Virsen was filled with deep anguish. He felt that since he had saved the king, he had fulfilled his duty. So he too, gave up his life.

Soon the news reached the king. He felt guilty for being the cause of so many deaths. So he too killed himself.

Then, Betal said, "Tell me, oh king, whose sacrifice was the greatest? Speak now or else, your head will be blown up into a thousand pieces."

"The king's sacrifice was the greatest of all," said Vikram, confidently. "He needn't have given up his life for his servant. Virsen was only doing his duty. All of them gave up their lives for their loved ones."

Just as Vikram ended his speech, Betal flew away and hung himself upside down on the peepul tree.

The Measure of Talent

King Vikram remembered his promise and was very determined not to return empty-handed to the sage. He purposefully walked back to the peepul tree, got the corpse down, slung it across his shoulders and walked on. Betal too, would not give up his storytelling.

Once upon a time, there lived two very talented brothers. They served their king in a very unusual way.

The elder one had the gift of judging a person by just looking at the person and instantly sensing any kind of hidden danger, while the younger one was gifted with a sharp sense of smell. He could tell just by smelling, where the object came from, and to whom it belonged.

One day, two men were passing through the forest nearby. They came to the court and requested the king to resolve their dispute over a valuable emerald necklace. The king wished to impress his subjects with

his justice and so he asked the two brothers to sort out the matter between them at once. The younger brother smelt their hands and within seconds,

he declared to whom the necklace actually belonged. The king was very impressed.

Some days later, the king was invited by the neighbouring ruler to visit his kingdom. The king accepted the invitation of the neighbouring king, but he got very worried and suspicious at the same time. He knew there had to be some motive behind the invitation, especially when the two kings did not get along well. After thinking for a while, he decided to take the two brothers along with him, to avoid any danger.

When the king reached his neighbour's kingdom, he was given a warm and grand welcome. A lavish meal was prepared for him and he was given many gifts. The two kings exchanged many valuable presents. After a magnificent reception, he was taken to a beautifully furnished room to rest.

Just when the king was about to lie down on his bed, the elder brother stopped him.

He warned the king that there was a nail hidden in the mattress. After a thorough search, he found that a nail was indeed stuck there. Then, the king asked the younger brother to examine the nail. When the younger brother smelt the nail, he said that it was poisonous. If the nail had pierced the king, he would have been killed instantly.

As usual, at the end of the story, Betal had a question to ask. He turned to Vikram and asked him, "Which one of the brothers was more talented? If you do not speak in spite of knowing the answer, I will burst your head into pieces."

"You are up to your old tricks again. You force me to speak, so that you can fly away from me. But since you have asked me, I must give the reply. I think the elder one was more talented than the younger brother.

This is because he could feel the presence of the nail but it was only after the nail was detected, could the younger brother use his sense of smell to tell that it was poisonous." said Vikram.

"You are absolutely right," said Betal, with a wicked grin. "But I must take leave of you, as you have spoken again."

Then, Betal flew away to the peepul tree and hung himself upside down on it.

The Ungrateful King

King Vikram walked back to the peepul tree patiently. He pulled the corpse down again. He knew he had to fulfil the sage's request. So with Betal slung over his shoulder, he continued walking towards the cremation ground where the sage was waiting for him. Betal started narrating another story to help pass the time pleasantly.

Once there lived a prince who had two very close friends. One was a soldier and the other was a scholar.

One day, the three friends went hunting together in the forest. Suddenly, a tiger appeared and sprang at the prince. His soldier friend immediately stepped forward and killed the tiger. After this incident, the

prince was grateful to his friend for saving his life.

Some time later, the prince came upon a wounded panther. He was terrified. So the young scholar killed the panther. At that time, the soldier friend was nowhere nearby.

When they reached the palace, the prince recounted the events to the king who was so happy and relieved to see his son alive that he decided to celebrate. He announced a rich reward for the scholar. But, there was no reward for the soldier who had also saved the prince's life. All were puzzled by the king's lack of gratitude to the soldier.

Then Betal asked, "Why did the king forget the warrior who saved his son?"

"Well, the soldier's duty is to guard the prince," said Vikram, "and he failed when the prince was attacked the second time. The king rightly rewarded the scholar, who risked his life to save the prince despite being untrained."

After listening to Vikram, Betal flew back to the tree and hung himself.

The Sage's Payment

After catching Betal once again, King Vikram walked on, and Betal continued with his storytelling.

Once there lived a king in a far-off kingdom. He was very ambitious for his only son. He wanted him to receive the best education, so that he would grow up to be a fine young man. With great difficulty, the king found a sage who had the reputation of being a good teacher.

He went to the sage and spoke very rudely. He forced him to accept his son as his student. He also told him, firmly, that his son should be treated as a prince ought to be treated.

The king's rude and arrogant attitude annoyed the sage. He rebuked the king saying, "In a school, all students are treated alike. No one is given special treatment. Therefore, the prince too will be treated like everyone else here."

The king was stunned by the sage's audacity. He controlled his anger then, but decided to punish him later. So leaving his son behind, he returned to his palace.

The school was situated in the forest. It was a serene and quiet place. The prince grew up in this atmosphere. He was a good student and made fast progress.

When he was sixteen years old, the prince decided to take leave of his teacher. Before leaving, the prince begged the sage to tell him what he could give him as *guru dakshina* for the years of love and guidance that he had bestowed on him.

Since the prince was persistent, the sage finally gave in and said that he would accept some payment definitely but later on. The prince was relieved to hear this.

Now the king had still not forgotten the the sage's behaviour. For all those years, he had been seething in anger and waiting patiently for his son to complete his education, so that he could avenge the insult.

The king decided to put his plan into action. Without wasting any more time, he sent his soldiers to the forest and told them to burn the school down.

After a few weeks, the prince was supposed to get married. He decided to go and seek his teacher's blessings.

On reaching there, to his horror, he saw his school reduced to ashes. "How could anyone do this?" asked the prince. "I will not rest till I have the head of the person who made you suffer."

The sage knew very well who the culprit was. In fact, he thought that now was the time to ask for the fee.

Then Betal asked Vikram, "What do you think the sage asked for?"

Vikram said, "He asked the prince to forgive his father. This shows that the sage was truly wise and not after revenge."

"True again! Your judgement is amazing," said Betal, admiringly. "But sadly, I will have to go, as you have spoken again."

Then he flew back to the peepul tree.

Valour and Discretion

It was a cold, eerie night. But King Vikram bravely walked back to the peepul tree and caught Betal. He walked towards the cremation ground, where the sage awaited him, hoping that Betal would not make him speak.

But it was difficult to stop Betal as he began to relate another story.

One day, Manohar, a poor boy, went hunting in the forest. Suddenly, he heard the loud screams of a woman. He became curious and walked stealthily towards the direction of the scream.

He saw a young woman being chased by a wild animal. Manohar bravely sprang forward and pulled her away from its path. Then he turned towards the wild animal and killed it with a single blow.

Now the woman he had saved was actually a princess. The princess took Manohar to her palace and told her father, the king, about his brave deed. The grateful king gave Manohar a high position in his army.

Now the king fought in many battles bravely. In one battle, Manohar saved the king's life by shielding him from a spear. People praised his bravery. If an impossible task came up, Manohar would do it.

Some time after Manohar got married, the kingdom was attacked by a gang of robbers who robbed and killed travellers. There was widespread discontentment in the kingdom.

The king consulted his ministers, but they too were afraid and hoped that Manohar would get rid of the thieves. But surprisingly he asked for the army's help.

Then Betal asked, "Why did Manohar lose courage?"

"It's simple," said Vikram, confidently. "Manohar was always brave. But once he got married, his priorities had changed. His family was dependent on him. So he could not take risks."

With this, Betal flew away to his abode.

The Shadow of Death

Vikram purposefully walked back, undeterred by Betal's behaviour. He pulled Betal down, and set off. Betal narrated another story, as he disliked the silence.

Once there lived a hard working, poor man. He dreamt of becoming rich one day. A sage had prophesied his future. He had said that he would never be rich in his life: he would live and die in poverty, irrespective of how hard he worked.

Moreover, the sage said that if he ever became rich, he would die soon after.

This upset the man. His enthusiasm to work hard and to become rich was completely dashed. He felt that all his hard work was useless. But old habits die hard. He continued to struggle.

One day, while he was cutting wood he found a big wooden chest filled with silver and gold coins. He stood dumbstruck.

It had enough money to sustain him for life. He got very excited at this thought.

Just when he was about to carry the chest home, he remembered the sage's prophecy. He was reluctant to take the chest away. But then he reasoned that if he left the chest in the forest, it would be of no use to anyone. He thought that he could do so much with it, even if he had to die soon.

With this thought in mind, he carried the chest to his village. There he used all the money for improving his village, which soon prospered.

"Now, tell me Vikram," said Betal, "how come the sage's words did not come true, as the poor man lived for so long?

Remember, if you don't speak, your head will burst into pieces."

"The answer is quite simple," said Vikram. "You see, the poor man worked hard for his village. So, the sage's words were true. The poor man made the village rich, but never became rich himself."

Hearing Vikram's verdict, Betal once again flew away to the peepul tree.

The Three Suitors

Once more, Vikram grabbed Betal, slung him across his shoulder, and started walking out of the forest. To pass the time, Betal related another story.

There once lived a very rich man who had a beautiful daughter, Manushree. When Manushree was old enough to get married, her father started looking for a suitable husband for her.

He finally narrowed down his choice to three good suitors.

Then her father asked Manushree to choose one suitor. The tension of choosing was quite a strain on her. As a result of thinking too much, she fell into a trance and died. When the news reached the three suitors, they were heartbroken. They decided to devote the rest of their lives to her memory.

One of the suitors took some of her ashes and immersed them in the Ganga.

He then started living on the banks of that river. The second suitor decided to lie down on her ashes, at the same place where she was cremated. The third became a nomad. He roamed from one place to another.

During the course of his journey, a holy couple gave him shelter. While staying with them, he witnessed a strange sight. The lady, while cooking, fell into the fire and died. The old man calmly collected her ashes, said a prayer, sprinkled some holy water, and lo and behold, she came back to life!

The young man was at once reminded of the beautiful Manushree. He thought that he too, could bring her back to life by reciting the same prayer.

After learning the prayer from the old man, he returned to the exact place where Manushree was cremated. Here, he met the other suitor who lived with her ashes.

After reciting the prayer, the suitor who lived on the banks of the River Ganga sprinkled some holy water on the ashes, and behold, there stood the beautiful Manushree.

All of them were thrilled to see Manushree again. But soon enough, a dispute broke out amongst them as to who would be the ideal husband for her. Each one of them thought that he was the most deserving candidate.

Ending the story thus, Betal asked Vikram, "Now tell me, which young man was the ideal suitor for the girl? If you keep quiet irrespective of knowing the answer, I will burst your head into a thousand pieces."

Without hesitation, Vikram replied, "To begin with, the suitor who gave Manushree life by reciting a prayer was like her father. The suitor who immersed her ashes in the river was like her mother. But the suitor who slept on her ashes, after sacrificing everything in life, is rightfully her husband."

"You are right!" cried Betal. "But you have spoken, so here I go."